Gigi's
COMEDY HOUR
A Fingerlings Joke Book

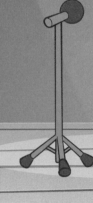

by Brian Elling

PENGUIN YOUNG READERS LICENSES

An Imprint of Penguin Random House LLC, New York

Additional illustrations by Shane L. Johnson

Fingerlings® and all product names, designations, and logos are trademarks of WowWee Group Limited. Copyright © 2016–2019 WowWee Group Limited. All rights reserved. Published in 2019 by Penguin Young Readers Licenses, an imprint of Penguin Random House LLC, New York. Manufactured in China.

Visit us online at www.penguinrandomhouse.com.

ISBN 9781524793630   10 9 8 7 6 5 4 3 2 1

Where does Polly the panda like to go scuba diving?

The Great *Bear*-ier Reef!

What did Polly the panda say after she got a splinter?
"I got a *bamboo-boo!*"

What's the Glitter Girls' favorite horror movie?
Franken-shine!

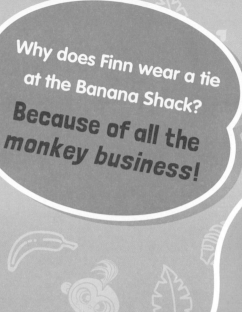

Why does Finn wear a tie at the Banana Shack? **Because of all the monkey business!**

Knock, knock!
Who's there?
Bella.
Bella who?
Bell–a doesn't work, so I had to knock!

What musical instrument does Marge the sloth like to play?

The *slowwww*-boe!

What type of monkey can float in the air?

A helium *baboon*!

Why do Fingerlings giraffes always know the weather?

Because their heads are *in the clouds*!

Where do the Minis like to go on vacation?

***Mini*-sota!**

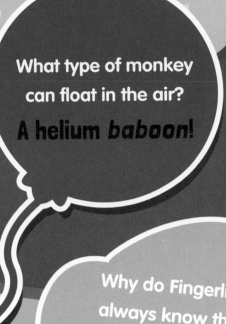

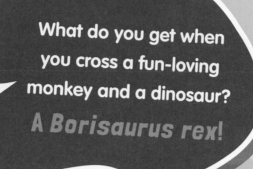

What do you get when you cross a fun-loving monkey and a dinosaur? *A Borisaurus rex!*

Why did Drew the panda climb down the tree when he heard a strange noise?

To get to the *root* of the problem!

How do the Minis get to school? In a *Mini*-van!

Knock, knock!

Who's there?

Skye.

Skye who?

Skye's getting cloudy. Open the door before my unicorn horn gets soaked!

Why are the sparkly Fingerlings so good at recycling?

Because they always pick up their *glitter*!

What type of train does Marge the sloth like to ride?

A *slow-comotive*!

Which Fingerling is the scariest? **Booo–ris!**

What tool did Finn use to fix the bathroom sink? A *monkey* wrench!

Why did Tara the dragon sing at the concert?

It was a *roar* opportunity!

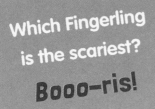

What do you call a Fingerling who likes to fly airplanes?

A *Winger-ling!*

Why does Meadow the giraffe only wear pants? Because giraffes don't like *shorts!*

Why are the Fingerlings dragons good at weighing things? Because of all their *scales!*

Why did Gray the elephant run away with the other elephants?

He thought he _herd_ something.

If Boris had a crown, what would he be called?

A Finger-king!

What did Kingsley the sloth say when he built a new hut in the treehouse?

"I'm branching out!"

How do the Fingerlings get on the Internet in their treehouse?
By *logging* on!
What did the giraffe say when she passed the ball to her teammate?
"Heads up!"
Knock, knock!
Who's there?
Noa.
Noa who?
Noa way I'm leaving until I meet a dragon!

Where do baby pandas keep their toys?

In their *cub*-by!

Why does Tara the dragon make so much noise when she walks?

Because she's always *dragon* her feet!

What did Noa the dragon say when she got a birthday present? **"This is fang-tastic!"**

Why did the librarian tell the banana cone to be quiet? **Because you're not supposed to yell-ow in the library.**

Why didn't Marge the sloth eat her french fries? **Because it was fast food!**

What did Kayla put on her paws when she used the punching bag?

Her *fox*-ing gloves.

What does Meadow the giraffe use to draw a map?

***Gir–aph* paper!**

Where do the Minis live?

In a condo–*Mini*–um!

What board game do bananas like to play?
Fruits and Ladders!

Knock, knock!
Who's there?
Candi.
Candi who?
Candi door be unlocked? This monkey wants to party!

Why did the Banana Shack stay closed all day?
It wasn't *peeling* very well.

BANANA SHACK

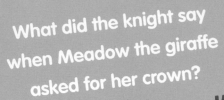

What did the knight say when Meadow the giraffe asked for her crown? **"Yes, your highness!"**

What do you get when you cross a beehive and a whole lot of cute monkeys? **Finger-stings!**

Knock, knock!

Who's there?

Razz.

Razz who?

Razz-a-cadabra! **Watch this monkey magically open the door!**

What does Gigi like to eat when she's at a picnic? **Uni-corn on the cob!**

Why are some dragons green? **They're not ripe yet!**

Why did Drew go shopping for new clothes?

His closet was totally *bear*!

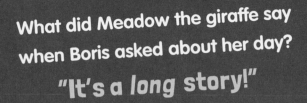

What did Meadow the giraffe say when Boris asked about her day? **"It's a long story!"**

Where does Mikey the fox like to watch TV?

In the *den*.

Why did the Fingerlings monkey hold on to the banana? **He wasn't Finn-ished with it yet!**

What's Bella's favorite rock band?

The Finger-*sings*!

How did the panda win the race?

Just *bear*-ly!

What do monkeys like to read at the library?

Furry tales!

What do you get when you cross Meadow the giraffe and a race with two winners?

A *neck*-tie!

What does Polly wear when she plays tennis?

A *pandanna*!

What did Gray the elephant say to the tree?

Nice *trunk*!

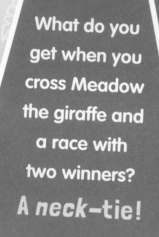

What did Bella say to her brother Boris when she beat him in a race?

You *twin* some, you lose some!

Why did the Glitter Girl pass the lifeguard test?

She was a very good *shimmer*!

Where do unicorns like to leave their cars?

Parkle Heights!

YAAAAAAAAY! It's time for . . . the *Glitter Girls*!

I love them so much it's driving me GLITTERALLY INSANE!!!!! So much glam! So much sparkle! So many funny jokes! And they can sing them all in perfect harmony!

Sing it, sisters!

Ahhhhhh!

Ahhhhhh!

Ahhhhhh!

Ahhhhhh!

Why did Mikey the fox look so suspicious?

He thought he was being *tailed*!

What did the little Fingerling say when he fell down?

I hurt *Mi-knee*!

What do you get when you cross Sloth Beach and Marge's birthday party?

A *shell*-ebration!

What's black and white and red all over?

A panda who likes strawberry jam!

What did Marge the sloth say when she found out she won an award?

"SLOW.M.G!"

Why did Boris miss Tara at the mall?

She was *dra*-gone already when he got there.

How did Lil' G get across the ocean?

On a *gir*-raft!

Why did Drew go to college?

To ex-*panda* his mind!

What do you get when you cross a giant hand and some coconuts?

A *palm* tree!

Where do giraffes learn geometry?
In *high* school.

Why are the Minis never on time?
Because they're always a *little* late!

Knock, knock!

Who's there?

Rose.

Rose who?

Rose early today to meet a glitter monkey!

Knock, knock!

Who's there?

Lexi.

Lexi who?

Lexi if this dragon can get the door open!

What do you get when you cross Bella the monkey and a traffic cone?

An *orange-utan!*

What did Marge say when she brought Boris his mail?

"*Not-so-speedy* delivery!"

Where does Polly like to go on vacation?
Ja-*panda*!

What is the Minis' favorite phrase?

***Small*'s well that ends well!**

Why did the Glitter Girl need help making friends?

Because she's so shy-ny.

Why did the pink Fingerling go to the doctor?

Because she had a *Bella*-ache!

Why did the dragon lose his job?

He got *fired*!

What does Gray like to use to stay cool?

An *ele*-fan!

What month do monkeys like best?

Ape-ril!

Why do Minis score well on tests?

They have great *short*-term memories!

Where does Kayla the fox keep her school lunch?

In her *cub*-by!

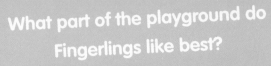

What part of the playground do Fingerlings like best?

The *monkey* bars!

Knock, knock!

Who's there?

Alika.

Alika who?

***Alika* to come play with the other unicorns!**

Why did Mikey want to stay indoors?

He didn't want to be *outfoxed*!

Why did Polly the panda climb the mountain by herself?

She's very inde-*pandant*!

What topping do the Glitter Girls put on their cupcakes?

Chocolate twinkles!

Knock, knock!
Who's there?
Monkey.
Monkey who?
Mon-key is missing. Open the door, Gigi!

What do you call
a Mini on her
thirteenth birthday?
A *teeny-ager*!

What did Gemma
the unicorn say
when the Mini took
her banana cone?

Hoof do
you think
you are?

Why did the girl
have to get a bigger
tree for all her tiny
Fingerlings?
Because she had
so *Mini* of them!